W9-ARD-726

POACHER PANIC

J. BURCHETT & S. VOGLER

STONE ARCH BOOKS
a capstone imprint

Wild Rescue books are published by Stone Arch Books
A Capstone Imprint
1710 Roe Crest Drive,
North Mankato, Minnesota 56003
www.capstonepub.com

First published by Stripes Publishing Ltd.
1 The Coda Centre
189 Munster Road
London SW6 6AW
© Jan Burchett and Sara Vogler, 2012
Interior Art © Diane Le Feyer of Cartoon Saloon, 2012

Library of Congress Cataloging-in-Publication Data
Burchett, Jan.
[Poacher peril]
Poacher panic / written by Jan Burchett [and] Sara Vogler ; illustrated by Diane
Le Feyer ; cover illustration by Sam Kennedy.
p. cm. -- (Wild rescue)
Originally published under the title Poacher peril. London : Stripes, 2009.
ISBN 978-1-4342-3286-1 (library binding)   ISBN 978-1-4342-4195-5 (pbk.)
1. Twins--Juvenile fiction. 2. Brothers and sisters--Juvenile fiction. 3. Sumatran
tiger--Juvenile fiction. 4. Wildlife conservation--Indonesia--Sumatra--Juvenile
fiction. 5. Poaching--Indonesia--Sumatra--Juvenile fiction. 6. Sumatra
(Indonesia)--Juvenile fiction. 7. Adventure stories. [1. Twins--Fiction. 2. Brothers
and sisters--Fiction. 3. Tiger--Fiction. 4. Wildlife conservation--Fiction. 5.
Poaching--Fiction. 6. Adventure and adventurers--Fiction. 7. Sumatra (Indonesia)-
-Fiction. 8. Indonesia--Fiction.] I. Vogler, Sara. II. Le Feyer, Diane, ill. III.
Kennedy, Sam, 1971- ill. IV. Title.
PZ7.B915966Pn 2012
823.914--dc23   2011025524

Cover Art: Sam Kennedy
Graphic Designer: Russell Griesmer
Production Specialist: Michelle Biedscheid

Design Credits: Shutterstock 51686107 (p. 4-5),
Shutterstock 51614464 (p. 148-149, 150, 152)

Printed in China by Nordica
1114/CA21401697
102014   008591R

TABLE OF CONTENTS

WILD RESCUE

MISSION

BEN WOODWARD
WILD Operative

ZOE WOODWARD
WILD Operative

BRIEFING

TARGET: ◎

CODE NAME: TORA

CHAPTER 1

WILD

"This is the weirdest present I've ever gotten!" said Ben.

A shiny glass eyeball was glaring up at him from its brown envelope.

"The weirdest present *we've* ever had. It's my birthday too," his twin sister Zoe reminded him. "Who's it from?"

"Dunno," said Ben. He shook the eyeball out of the envelope. It was the size of a small marble with a black dot in the center and yellow flecks outside.

Zoe took the envelope and pulled out a piece of paper with a printed message.

"Happy Eleventh Birthday, Zoe and Ben," she read. "But it's not signed."

"This is one of your jokes, isn't it?" Ben asked. He grinned, waving the marble in her face.

His sister shook her head. "I don't know anything about it," she said.

"Yeah, right!" Ben said.

"Honest!" insisted Zoe. "I've never seen it before."

"Maybe Mom and Dad sent it," suggested Ben.

"We got their presents already," said Zoe. She carefully studied the stamp on the envelope. "Anyway, this letter didn't come from Mexico."

Ben and Zoe's parents were veterinarians who traveled the world working with endangered animals. A month ago they'd been sent to Mexico to help protect the critically endangered Chiapan Climbing Rat.

In the past, Ben and Zoe had always gone with their parents. But this September, they would be starting school again, so their parents decided they couldn't go to Mexico. Their parents kept them updated on their adventures with regular phone calls, but it just wasn't the same as actually being there. Grandma was taking care of them while their parents were gone. Right now, she was in the kitchen, frosting a birthday cake.

Ben held up the eyeball. "Maybe it's a clue to something," he said. "Like in those treasure hunts Mom and Dad used to do for us."

"It's not much of a clue, though," said Zoe, frowning. "What do we do next?"

"Maybe the sender left a message on our blog," said Ben. "That's how most people get in touch with us!" He pocketed the glass eyeball, went to the computer, and logged in. A picture of a gorilla filled the screen. The words "animals in danger" arched over its head. The deep cry of a silverback male echoed through the room.

During their travels with their parents Ben and Zoe regularly posted updates of their projects on their website. They also used the site to keep in touch with the people they'd met all over the world.

"There's tons of new emails," said Ben. He scrolled down. "There's one from the Elephant Sanctuary in Kenya."

Zoe's eyes lit up. "Open it!" she said.

Ben clicked on the email and a
picture of a baby elephant popped up.
"Aww," Zoe purred. "Zahara had a bull calf
this morning!"

Ben rolled his eyes and quickly scrolled
down the list. He was just as passionate
about protecting animals as his sister, but
sometimes she was kind of annoying.

"There's one from Brian and his orangutans," Ben told Zoe.

"I don't recognize the one below it," said Zoe. "It says 'The Island'."

Ben clicked on it. "By now, you'll have the eye," he read slowly. "Time to give it back to its rightful owner so the adventure can begin."

"'Adventure'?" repeated Zoe. "What adventure?"

Ben pulled the eyeball out of his pocket. "Looks like we have to find this thing's owner," he said. "But who's missing a glass eye?"

"It looks like a cat's eye," said Zoe.

"It's not," Ben said. "They don't have round pupils like this." Suddenly he ran for the door. "I know!"

Zoe caught up with him by the bookshelf in the hall. He was wobbling on a chair, reaching for the very top. He pulled down an ugly china tiger that Grandma had brought when she came to stay with them.

The tiger was battered and chipped and had one yellow glass eye. The other was missing, leaving only an empty socket.

Ben looked at Zoe. "So . . . did Grandma make this puzzle?" he asked.

"Put it in and we'll find out," urged Zoe.

Ben pressed the eyeball into the socket. It fit perfectly.

There was a loud click. Then a three-dimensional image of a man appeared in front of them.

"A hologram!" said Zoe.

"Greetings, my nephew and niece," said the image. "Of course, if you're not Ben and Zoe Woodward, then this message isn't for you."

"It's Uncle Stephen!" said Ben. "But he disappeared four years ago."

Their uncle, Dr. Stephen Fisher, was a world-renowned animal specialist. He vanished around the time of their seventh birthday and hadn't been seen since. Ben and Zoe missed their uncle. They'd loved his crazy ways. He had always made up clever games that had them thinking hard and howling with laughter at the same time.

"I'm sorry for disappearing some time ago," said the flickering image. "This is my hologram. But don't worry, I'm not dead — far from it, in fact. I went undercover so I could concentrate on my great plan to save endangered animals."

The image stepped closer to them. "I'm going to tell you a secret," he said. He looked around as if to make sure no one was listening. Ben and Zoe found themselves doing the same. "Four years ago, I set up an organization called WILD. This must remain completely confidential!"

"Why's he telling us about it, then?" whispered Ben.

"I bet you're wondering why I'm telling you about it," Uncle Stephen said, grinning. Ben smiled back. "I've kept an eye on you two and I'm very impressed with your work with endangered animals," Stephen said. "You both have valuable skills and knowledge. I want you to join me at WILD. Can't tell you where it is, of course, but your contact will be in touch shortly. See you soon!"

The image flickered, then disappeared.

"Wow!" whispered Ben. "Uncle Stephen wants us to join his secret organization! We'd better pack."

"Hold on," said Zoe. "You're always rushing into things. We don't know where we're going yet, or who our contact is."

"Children!" Grandma yelled from the kitchen. "Your birthday cake is ready!"

"We'll talk later," said Ben. "Chocolate cake takes priority!"

They raced down the hall to the kitchen. They found Grandma standing in the doorway, smiling at them. She held out a chocolate cake with eleven candles.

"Just finished this, in time for your WILD adventure," she said with a wink.

CHAPTER 2

HEADQUARTERS

Ben and Zoe bumped up and down in the back seat of Grandma's little car as she drove.

"I don't get it, Grandma," said Ben. "You were in on Uncle Stephen's secret all along?"

"Of course," Grandma said.

"Then can you tell us more about WILD?" Zoe asked.

"Certainly not!" said Grandma. "That's up to Stephen."

Grandma suddenly steered the car off the road and drove across a field! The car was lurching wildly over the bumpy ground.

Zoe looked at Ben. "Has Grandma gone nuts?" she whispered.

"Almost there," called their grandmother over her shoulder.

Zoe and Ben could see a helicopter in the field ahead. A young woman jumped out. She was wearing jeans and a thick jacket. Her blonde hair was tied in a rough ponytail.

Grandma bumped the car to a halt and pointed at the woman. "That's Erika," she said. "She'll be taking you from here. Have fun and be safe — and don't worry about your mom and dad. I'll deal with them."

"See you soon!" Grandma called back as she hurtled away across the field.

"This is so unreal!" Zoe muttered as the woman walked up to shake their hands.

"Good morning, Ben and Zoe," the woman said in a German accent. "I'm Erika Bohn, Dr. Fisher's second-in-command. I'm here to take you to the Island."

Erika led them
to the helicopter and
settled herself in the pilot's
seat. "Strap yourselves in," she
said.

Erika put on her headset and handed
Ben and Zoe some ear protectors. She
began flicking switches. The door closed
and the rotors roared to life.

"Where are we going?" asked Ben,
shouting above the noise.

"Any questions will have to wait for Dr.
Fisher," Erika told them as they flew north.

Erika continued speaking as they flew over fields and towns. "Stephen can't wait to tell you all about it himself. He would never forgive me if I let anything slip."

Zoe sniffed the air. "What's that smell? Is everything all right with the helicopter?"

Erika chuckled. "I forgot to warn you. We use alternative energy sources here. WILD's helicopter is fueled by chicken manure."

"Manure?" repeated Ben. "Wait, you mean . . ."

"Yep — chicken poop!" said Erika, chuckling. "It's environmentally friendly, free, and there's plenty on the Island. But it does take a while to get used to the smell."

That gave Ben and Zoe a lot to think about. Before they knew it, the helicopter was flying over choppy waves.

"Landing in thirty seconds," Erika announced.

"Where?" whispered Zoe.

"There's a little island ahead," Ben told her, looking out of his window.

Ben frowned. "But that can't be it," he added. "It looks too small."

Erika brought the helicopter down on a bare patch of dirt among wild grass and bushes. Ben and Zoe jumped down and gazed at their desolate surroundings. Erika appeared at their side. She pulled a remote control from her jacket and pressed a button. Sheets of old wood suddenly rose from the ground around the helicopter and made a shelter. A corrugated roof slid up from one of the walls and slammed down on top.

"Now no one will know there's a helicopter there," Erika explained. "It's important for WILD to stay under the radar."

Erika walked ahead, stepping carefully around piles of animal droppings.

"Follow me, and watch your step," Erika warned. "There's 'fuel' everywhere."

They were walking through what looked like a chicken farm. There were many hens and chickens running around freely.

"It looks like a mess," said Erika, "but that's all part of WILD's disguise. I promise the chickens are happy here."

"Look at the chicks!" cooed Zoe, stopping to watch a mother hen stalk past, followed by her babies. "They're like little balls of fluff!"

"Cuteness overload," Ben said, pretending to gag. Zoe stuck out her tongue at him.

Erika flung open the door of a rickety old shed. There was an old-fashioned toilet inside. "In we go!" she said cheerfully.

Ben and Zoe looked uncomfortably at each other. They each knew what the other was thinking: this was getting really weird.

It was a tight squeeze, especially after Erika had pulled the door shut and closed the bolt. She pulled the toilet chain. Instead of the expected noise of water gurgling, there was a gentle electronic hum. "Hold on to your tummies," she warned. "This is a turbo elevator."

"Turbo —?!" Zoe's question was cut off when the elevator suddenly shot downward.

It raced downward at a breakneck pace. Several violent lurches later, it came to rest deep underground.

"That was better than any theme park ride!" Ben howled. Zoe, on the other hand, looked a little green as she silently stepped out.

"Welcome to WILD headquarters," said Erika. "We coordinate all of our plans here."

Zoe and Ben followed her into a long, brightly lit hallway. There were doors on both sides. Erika waved a hand at them as they walked past. "These are bedrooms, bathrooms, everything we need to live on an island."

She stopped at a door at the far end of the hall and placed her fingertips on an electronic pad. The words "CONTROL ROOM" were marked above the door.

"Print identification complete," chirped an electronic voice.

"This is like a spy movie," Zoe whispered to Ben. "What are we getting ourselves into?"

The door slid open. Erika ushered Zoe and Ben through and it closed silently behind them.

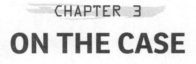

CHAPTER 3

ON THE CASE

Ben and Zoe stared open-mouthed at the huge, busy room in front of them. The walls were covered with giant plasma screens showing footage of animals in the wild. People sitting at computers looked up and smiled, then immediately went back to their work.

"They're all endangered," murmured Ben. He watched the amazing sight of mountain gorillas, pandas, and hawksbill turtles in their natural habitats on the many computer monitors.

Zoe gasped and pointed at one of the screens. "A panda bear!" she exclaimed. "They're an endangered species."

"You're right," said a deep voice. "And WILD's working hard to help protect the species from extinction."

Out from behind a workstation stepped Uncle Stephen. He was wearing faded jeans and sports coat with a bow tie. His spiky hair looked like it hadn't been combed in days.

"Ben and Zoe!" he said, smiling widely. "You haven't changed much from the seven-year-old scamps I remember," he went on. "There's still a thirst for adventure in those bright blue eyes of yours."

"It's great to see you again," said Zoe, giving him a hug.

Uncle Stephen laughed and ruffled her hair. "What do you think of WILD's headquarters?" he asked.

"Cool!" said Ben, looking around the busy room. "How deep underground are we?"

"Several hundred feet," Uncle Stephen replied. "It keeps us away from prying eyes. You'd be surprised how much space we have down here. There's this control room, and we also have offices, living quarters, labs, a games room, and even a pool."

"I can't imagine you organizing all this!" Zoe teased. "You used to forget your keys at our house every time you visited."

"You've got a point, Zoe," Uncle Stephen chuckled. "But thanks to Erika, WILD runs like clockwork. She's my second-in-command and keeps everything running smoothly. I just do some tinkering here and there."

Erika smiled. "I think you're being modest," she said. "After all, you are the driving force behind the entire operation. You plan all of our missions."

"Well, I suppose there is that," admitted Uncle Stephen.

"And you invent all the gadgets and equipment WILD uses," Erika went on.

"All environmentally friendly, of course," put in Uncle Stephen.

"Like the chicken-poop fuel," said Zoe. "What do you use the eggs for? Something really important?"

"Breakfast," Uncle Stephen said.

"There's one thing I don't understand," said Ben thoughtfully. "Why does WILD have to be secret? Couldn't you get more help if the organization was public?"

"We could," said Uncle Stephen. "But we'd get a lot more enemies, too. If nobody knows we exist, then we can operate without interference."

"Interference?" Zoe repeated. "Who would want to stop you from helping animals in danger?"

"Poachers, corrupt corporations, collectors, those who have their own plans for the animals' habitats. They'd all want to stop us," Erika explained. "So we must remain completely hidden from the world."

"As you can see, working for WILD can be dangerous at times," warned Uncle Stephen.

"Do you still want to take on your first mission?" their uncle asked.

"Mission?" Ben repeated, his eyes lighting up. "Us?"

"Of course," said Uncle Stephen. "WILD has a very important project — I can't think of anyone better than you two to take it on!"

"Count us in!" Zoe said. Ben nodded.

"Good!" Uncle Stephen said. He rubbed his hands together. "Now, one of WILD's planes will be ready first thing tomorrow. Erika will be your pilot again."

Erika cleared her throat. "You haven't told them where they're going yet," she said.

"Haven't I?" Uncle Stephen said He went over to a control panel and touched it. A world map appeared on the largest screen.

Uncle Stephen navigated it to the Indian Ocean and zoomed in on a long, thin island. "Sumatra," he said.

"Wow!" exclaimed Zoe. "What will we be doing there?"

"Your mission is to save a tiger," said Uncle Stephen. "Her name is Tora."

"Sumatran tigers are critically endangered," Ben piped up. "Because of poaching, there are only a few hundred left living freely in the wild."

"We know," whispered Zoe. "Stop showing off."

"Ben's right," said Uncle Stephen. He waved a hand toward a young man who was bent over a keyboard.

"That's James," Stephen said. "He intercepts Internet information about poaching."

James gave a quick nod and smiled at them.

"He found out that poachers are active around Aman Tempat, a village in the southwest," Uncle Stephen continued. "Last month they killed a male tiger, probably Tora's mate. Now Tora is being targeted by a rich collector who'll pay these poachers handsomely for her capture — and for her two newborn cubs. But we've got a little time. According to the information we've gathered, they're waiting for the cubs to be old enough to leave their den."

"When will that be?" asked Ben.

"Good question," said Uncle Stephen.

"We think she had the cubs about seven weeks ago," Uncle Stephen continued.

"They'll be leaving the den very soon, then," Zoe said. She sighed.

Her uncle nodded. "Indeed, Zoe. Tiger cubs usually emerge from their den at about two months old," he told them. "Your mission is to monitor the den and alert us as soon as they do. Then we can rescue them before the poachers can kidnap them."

"When the cubs are out, you'll make contact and we'll tell the nearby Kinaree Sanctuary," Erika added. "Anonymously, of course."

"And in the meantime, we'll try to find out more about this collector," said Uncle Stephen, looking stern for once. "She must be stopped."

"There's something I don't understand," said Ben. "Why are the poachers waiting for the cubs to come out of their den? Why don't they just go in and get them right now?"

"The collector told the poachers to wait," said Dr. Fisher solemnly. "She wants the cubs to be a certain size. She's going to have Tora and her cubs killed — and stuffed."

Ben and Zoe gasped.

"So you see how urgent this is," Uncle Stephen said. "Stay away from those poachers. They're dangerous! People like that will stop at nothing to get their money. Now, Erika, have I forgotten anything?"

"BUGs, Stephen?" Erika said.

The children exchanged puzzled looks.

"Of course!" said Uncle Stephen. "Silly me. You'll need your Brilliant Undercover Gizmos."

He yanked open a drawer and pulled out two things that looked like handheld gaming devices. "Found them!" he said. His face lit up with excitement as he handed them to Zoe and Ben.

"Cool," Ben said. He turned his BUG over in his hand. It was made of hard shiny black plastic, and had a small screen with lots of buttons. "What does it do?"

"They're my latest invention," Stephen explained. "They're solar-powered and they recharge themselves automatically. They've got almost everything you'll need in one package: communicators, a translator, even tracking devices. And they flick back to an innocent-looking video game console if anyone comes along!"

"Let's go visit the storeroom," said Erika. "We have specially designed, lightweight backpacks that we can fill with everything you need."

Erika smiled. "By the way, are you up to date with your travel vaccinations?"

Ben nodded. "Yeah," he said. "Grandma insists on it. Now I know why!"

"Let me get this straight, Uncle Stephen," Zoe said. "You want me and Ben to go to the other side of the world to save a tiger and her cubs from dangerous poachers?"

"Yep!" declared their uncle. "You're perfect for the job. Who would suspect a couple of kids who seem to be on vacation? Meanwhile, you're both brave and smart and you know more about animals than anyone else I can think of. But most important of all — I can trust you both."

Their uncle paused for a moment. He frowned and looked at them earnestly. "But I suppose I should ask," he said, "will you do it?"

"YES!" shouted Ben and Zoe together.

CHAPTER 4

WICAKSONO

Zoe woke with a start. For a moment, she couldn't remember where she was. Then it came to her. It was hard to believe that only two days ago, they'd agreed to undertake the biggest adventure of their lives. And now, here they were on the other side of the world, in a little wooden hut in the steamy Sumatran rainforest. The excitement made her stomach flutter.

She tossed her sheets aside and swung her legs over the edge of the camp bed, tangling herself in the mosquito net that hung around it.

After a brief struggle, Zoe emerged from the net. She stared at the bed next to hers. Ben was still asleep.

Zoe walked over to his bed. "Wake up!" she said, shaking him through his bed's netting.

Ben grunted and turned over. Zoe sighed. Ben always suffered worse jet lag than she did whenever they traveled. They'd arrived at the hut late at night, after a long plane ride and a bumpy journey in a jeep. But now bright morning light was streaming in through the blinds.

Zoe padded around the room, feeling the rough mat under her bare feet. The place was simple. It was a single room with a cupboard, a one-burner stove, and a stone bowl — the toilet — in the corner.

Erika had left bottles of water and some fruit on a little table. She'd told them to tell anyone who asked that they were traveling with their aunt Erika, who liked to go off sightseeing on her own. Erika had certainly gone off on her own, but she wasn't sightseeing. By now, she was likely in Jakarta, Indonesia, following a lead on the rich collector.

Zoe pulled her crumpled clothes out of her backpack and got dressed. Grabbing a banana, she took her BUG outside. The hut was in a clearing near the village of Aman Tempat. The clearing was surrounded by lush green trees, and the air was full of bird songs and the scent of flowers. A blue-winged butterfly landed on the log next to her. Zoe saw that the midday sun was directly overhead. They had slept for hours.

"What did Erika say about using the BUGs?" Zoe said. She scrolled down the menu. "How does the Translator work?"

There was a small button on the side. It was made of a soft, squishy plastic, and came away in her hand. "An earpiece!" she exclaimed. She stuck it in her ear. It was so comfortable that she couldn't even feel it.

Inside the hut, Ben opened his eyes. He could hear Zoe muttering outside. "Communicator, satellite tracker . . ."

Ben popped his head out the door. "Morning!" he said.

"Afternoon, you mean!" Zoe said, grinning. "This little BUG gadget is amazing! I'm trying to remember everything Erika told us about it. I'd ask for your help, but I'm pretty sure you weren't listening to anything she said."

"No, I was," said Ben. "I remember
her saying we have to pretend to be on
vacation, and the local people are used to
tourists . . . and . . ." Ben trailed off.

"That's it?" said Zoe. "Figures. You were
too busy watching TV on the trip over."

"One of those TV shows told me a lot
about Sumatra," Ben argued.

Zoe just stuck out her tongue at him. "Get dressed," she said. "We need to go into the village and find out as much as we can about Tora. And we might be able to get a cellphone signal there."

Ben started walking away. "Remember to be careful," Zoe warned. "No one can know about our mission."

"My mission is to buy food," joked Ben.

Zoe sighed. "You always think with your stomach," she said.

As soon as Ben was ready, they set out on a narrow path. Soon, they found a little marketplace surrounded by houses.

All the houses had steeply curved roofs with carved points at each end. Several of them had storefronts. The place was total chaos.

Countless villagers called to them to come and see what they were selling.

"Erika was right," Zoe whispered to Ben. "They're used to tourists."

"They must be speaking Bahasa Indonesia," Ben whispered back.

"It sounds like English to me," Zoe said, smiling coyly.

Ben snorted. "No way!" he said. "I can't understand a word."

"Maybe you should clean your ears out," Zoe teased. "The lady at that stall with the bamboo baskets is saying she has the best rice, fish, and fruit in the village. Why aren't you buying some? You said you were hungry."

Ben looked completely confused. Zoe burst out laughing.

Making sure no one was watching, Zoe grabbed Ben's BUG and pulled off the earpiece that was hidden there.

"You were right, the language you're hearing is Bahasa Indonesia," she admitted. "And this is a translator. I'm using mine already. It makes the voices sound a little robotic, but I can understand everything they say. Here, stick it in your ear."

Ben shoved the earpiece in. "Lead me to the food!" he joked. "What's that awesome smell? It's coming from that shop."

Ben pointed to a large hut with wooden walls and a tin roof. A man was crouched over a small stove at the front, frying something in a pan. Ben grabbed Zoe's arm and dragged her toward it.

The shopkeeper looked up. "Banana fritters," he said in English, giving Ben and Zoe a broad grin. "We call them *godok pisang*."

"Don't need the translator here," Ben muttered. He pulled out the wallet full of rupiah that Erika had given them. "Five, please."

"Just one for me," added Zoe.

"You are Australian?" asked the man, ladling the sizzling fritters into a small bamboo bowl.

"No, we're from the United States," explained Zoe. "We're on vacation with our aunt."

The man nodded. "We have many visitors from overseas," he told them. "I am pleased to meet you. My name is Catur."

"I'm Ben," Ben said as he chewed. "This is my sister, Zoe. And this is a fantastic fritter!" The man nodded and smiled.

"It's nice here," Zoe told the storekeeper. "We can't wait to explore."

"There are good bus rides," Catur told them. "My brother-in-law is the driver."

"You can go as far as Gonglung," he added. "It's a big town."

"And what about this jungle?" said Ben, pointing at the dense wall of trees around the village. "We want to see some wildlife."

"Too dangerous to go on your own," said Catur. "Tell your aunt to keep you away from there. There are fierce animals in the jungle. Leopards, many wild cats, even a tiger."

Zoe nudged Ben's ankle with her foot. "A tiger?" she repeated. "We'll definitely stay away!"

Ben caught on to his sister's act. He pretended to be worried and afraid. "Does it come near the village?" he asked.

"If it did, you would not be in danger," said Catur, smiling. "We would set a trap."

Zoe gasped. "And kill it?" she asked.

"No," Catur said, smiling. "It would be taken to the Kinaree Tiger Sanctuary. It is a good place for tourists to go. Your aunt could take you. It is only a day's drive from here. Now, is there anything else you need? I have necklaces, scarves, many nice things for you to take home."

Zoe shook her head. "No, thank you," she said. But we'll be back for more godok pisang later!"

As Ben and Zoe continued through the village, they saw a man sitting outside on a porch, drinking from a bottle. He watched them coldly, rocking his chair on its back legs.

"He doesn't look very friendly," Zoe muttered.

Suddenly, three other men came up the steps of the porch. The man jumped up, glanced around suspiciously, and opened his door. The men all took off their shoes. Zoe turned up the sensitivity of her BUG and listened to the translated conversation.

"Keep it quiet, Wicaksono!" one of the newcomers said as he went inside. "No one must find out — especially my wife. She'll be really angry if she discovers what we're doing."

"The money is worth it," said the ragged man. "We're going to make a killing!"

All of them burst into laughter at the man's joke. The wooden door of the hut slammed behind them.

Zoe and Ben walked away to a safe distance. Zoe turned to her brother.

"He talked about making a killing and getting lots of money for it," Zoe whispered in alarm. "That Wicaksono man must be the poacher!"

"You're probably right," said Ben.

Zoe gasped. "And that means he's going after Tora!" she said.

CHAPTER 5

RECON

"Okay, so we found the poacher," said
Zoe, sitting under the shade of a palm tree
in the marketplace. "I know Uncle Stephen
said we had to stay away from poachers,
but he never said we couldn't keep an eye
on Wicaksono's activities. I mean, we need
to know what danger Tora's in, right?"

"Sure," said Ben with a grin. "Is
there something on the BUG that tracks
animals?"

"Of course," said Zoe, rolling her eyes.

"If you'd been listening to Erika, you'd know we can MARK Tora with a tiny microchip," Zoe explained. "She'll hardly feel it. But that doesn't help us now."

Ben grinned mischievously. "Really?"

"Wait a minute," said Zoe. "What are you planning? I can always tell you have some crazy idea when you smile like that."

"We could fire a tracking dart into Wicaksono," Ben said, smiling broadly. "And then follow him to find out what's going on," Ben added.

"Someone's coming!" hissed Zoe. She dragged Ben off between two of the houses. They could see the men talking on Wicaksono's porch. Ben got out his BUG and tapped in "tracking."

"You're finally getting the hang of it," whispered Zoe.

Ben didn't respond. A target ring was showing on his BUG's screen. Holding it up, he aimed it at Wicaksono's bare arm. Ben fired a dart with a *CLICK!*

Immediately, the man flinched and slapped his arm.

Zoe sighed with relief. "He thinks it's just a mosquito," she said.

"Shh," Ben warned. "If he sees or hears us, we're done for."

The man and his friends went back inside the house. Ben checked the screen. A satellite map of Aman Tempat came up and a green light pulsed where Wicaksono's house was. "It'll flash to warn us if he leaves the village," Ben said.

"What are you doing?" came a translated voice in their earpieces.

They looked up guiltily, then quickly pretended they had not understood. Zoe secretly clicked the screen of her BUG to game mode.

It was the woman who had been calling from her stall. She stared at them and the BUG, puzzled. Then she grinned. "You kids and your video games," she said in thickly accented English. "Where are your parents? I have food to sell."

"Our aunt is away for the day," said Zoe, "but we'll buy some food from you."

The woman beckoned to them and they followed her to her stall. "We're on vacation," Zoe told the woman. Ben eagerly inspected the baskets of brightly colored fruits.

Zoe pointed at her chest. "I'm Zoe," she said. Then she stuck her thumb out at Ben. "This is Ben, my brother. We're twins."

"I'm Angkasa," she said warmly. "It is nice to meet you."

"We're hoping to explore," said Zoe. "But people tell us the jungle is not safe." She hoped Angkasa might know more about Tora than Catur seemed to.

Angkasa nodded. "There are many stories about the jungle. There is a creature called *orang pendek*." Angkasa frowned. "People say he is a small man. Hairy and strong like five elephants. My father saw one, but not me."

"Cool," said Ben, forgetting about the food for a moment.

"My father saw it at Silent Water," Angkasa went on. "It is a watering hole in the jungle." She shivered. "We don't go there. It's an evil place."

"Do animals use it?" Zoe asked, glancing at Ben.

"Yes," said Angkasa. "But not people. Even poachers keep away, I think."

"Poachers!" exclaimed Zoe.

Angkasa nodded. "Poachers are not welcome in our village," she said. "There was a tiger eating our goats, so we told Kinaree Sanctuary and they got a trap ready. That way, the sanctuary comes and takes tiger to a safe place. But poachers got there first this time. Someone in the village helped them."

"Someone in the village?" gasped Zoe, pretending to be shocked by the revelation.

Angkasa lowered her voice. "A bad man." Her eyes flickered down the row of houses. Zoe was sure that she was looking at Wicaksono's house.

"He sells bones, animal skins, and other things that are against the law," said Angkasa. She looked around nervously as if she thought someone might be listening. "I have work to do," she said, hurriedly finding bags for the food Ben had chosen.

Ben and Zoe paid Angkasa and headed back to their hut. They said nothing until they were far away from the village.

"We're pretty good spies!" Ben laughed, punching Zoe's arm playfully. "We've pinpointed the poacher."

"Now we know where Tora goes to drink and hunt — Silent Water, and we've done it all in one afternoon," said Zoe, rubbing her arm. "Uncle Stephen will be proud of us."

"He sure will," said Ben.

Ben scrolled through the menu on his BUG and brought up a map of the area. "Silent Water's here," he murmured. "Tigers like to drink at night, so that's when we'll go there."

"It's a good place to start," agreed Zoe, "but I don't like the sound of it. What did she call that strange hairy man?"

"*Orang pendek*," Ben said. He grinned. "It's just a scary story. You know, like the Loch Ness monster or Bigfoot. Anyway, I'll protect you."

"You?" scoffed Zoe. "You'd be as useful as a concrete trampoline."

"Then don't come running to me when that pendek creature bites your legs off!" joked Ben. He ducked just as Zoe swiped at him.

"How's our poacher doing?" Zoe asked.

"He hasn't moved," said Ben, glancing at his BUG. "Besides, we don't have to worry about him until the cubs leave the den." "And we've got an advantage," said Zoe. "The poachers have no idea we're going to thwart their plans."

Ben gritted his teeth. "WILD to the rescue!"

CHAPTER 6
SILENT WATER

The twins sat on the floor of their hut, eating fish and rice from a papaya skin. "What time is it?" asked Ben.

"Late," said Zoe. "It'll be dusk soon. And darkness comes very quickly this near the equator."

Ben threw his papaya skin aside and pulled on his walking boots. "Let's go!" he said. "Tigers are nocturnal and usually hunt at night."

"Hang on a sec!" said Zoe. "We'll need supplies." She unzipped a small backpack from her big one and put water, fruit, and the medical kit inside.

Zoe checked the route on the BUG's satellite map. Then she plunged her hand into one of the backpack pockets. "We'll need the night-vision glasses Erika told us about," she said. "It'll be as dark as night underneath the trees."

2.25
phts

bat: 6.5

autonomy
high

21 h 256B light 66.54

Zoe handed Ben a pair. "These are state-of-the-art technology," she exclaimed.

Ben pulled them over his head and stared out into the gloom.

"The world's all green," he said. He turned a dial on the nosepiece. "Awesome, they've got telephoto lenses. I can zoom right in."

"This is going to be hard work," Zoe said, pushing aside branches.

As their footsteps crunched on the dead leaves of the forest floor they heard the warning cries of unseen animals. But they moved on, keeping their footsteps as quiet as possible. After a while, Zoe stretched up and ran her hand over the bark of a tree.

"This is no time for nature studies!" Ben whispered to her.

"But this is important," insisted Zoe. "Look." Four deep vertical gashes ran down the trunk. Light wood could be seen underneath.

"Wow," Ben said. "Those are tiger claw marks — and they look fresh."

"Well, duh," Zoe said with a sigh. "Erika said she's the only tiger in the area, so they have to be Tora's." She looked around. "Her footprints must be here somewhere . . ."

A sudden shriek from high in the trees broke the silence. They froze. Zoe's BUG vibrated in her hand. "Phew!" she whispered. "It analyzed the sound. It was just a tarsier monkey."

"I wasn't worried," Ben said, composing himself. Zoe rolled her eyes.

They walked on, carefully watching every movement from the undergrowth, pausing only when a spiky little creature scurried past.

"That's a brush-tailed porcupine," Zoe told Ben. "Wish we had time to study the wildlife."

They came to a narrow clearing through the trees, where large animals had broken away the vegetation to make a path. Ben bent to examine the ground.

"We're on her trail," he said, pointing at a paw print. "This must be the way she comes to drink."

Zoe bent down to look. There on the soft earth was a large paw print next to four smaller ones.

"I thought they'd be more like circles," said Zoe, puzzled.

"That's the males," said Ben. "Female tigers have uneven paws. It's got to be Tora's!"

Zoe checked her satellite map.

"Looks like this path heads straight to Silent Water," Zoe said. "Cool! We're taking the same track as she did."

They followed the trail through the trees for almost an hour, heading deeper and deeper into the jungle.

Zoe suddenly clutched Ben's arm. "What?" Ben whispered.

"Dunno," said Zoe. "I've just got a sort of creepy feeling. Remember what Angkasa said about Silent Water. What if that orang-thingy shows up?"

Ben grabbed Zoe by the hand and pulled her along.

"There won't be anything like that there," Ben said, sounding braver than he felt. "It's just a story the locals made up to scare tourists."

A screech split the air and echoed eerily. "It's a tarsier," said Ben quickly, as he felt Zoe tense and pull back. "We've heard them before. In Thailand, remember?"

Ben knew the best thing to do when Zoe was frightened was to keep her focused on something else. "Hey, I can see water through the trees!" Ben announced.

Zoe looked. "Oooh," Zoe cooed. "That must be Silent Water!"

Just beyond them, the trees gave way to a flat and glimmering moonlit pool. It was surrounded by tall, overhanging trees and a tangle of bushes.

A fallen tree rested in the pool and large rocks were scattered around the bank. There was no sign of Tora the tiger.

"It really is silent," Ben said. "There must be some animals around here, but it's like everything's just completely still."

Suddenly, they heard something moving through the trees on the other side of the waterhole.

Zoe dragged Ben down behind a thick, fern-like bush to the side of the trail. "What's that?" she whispered.

With a cracking of branches underfoot, a solid black shape ambled into the clearing. The moonlight illuminated its leathery back.

"If that's an *orang pendek*, I'm a dung beetle," whispered Ben.

"It's a Sumatran rhino!" said Zoe, her fear forgotten. "There are hardly any left in the wild. Look at his cute little face."

"They might look cute, but they can be dangerous," warned Ben. "If that charged at us, we'd be done for."

They watched as the heavy, slow-moving rhinoceros lowered its head to the water. Its long, hairy ears twitched as it drank.

"Poachers kill them for their horns," Zoe whispered. "We should tell Uncle Stephen that there are some here."

Zoe and Ben stood and watched. Bit by bit, Silent Water came alive. Deer, wild pigs, and tapirs emerged to drink and swim. After a while, Zoe checked the time. To her amazement, two hours had passed since they'd found the waterhole.

"I'm getting sore feet," moaned Ben. "I've never stood still for so long."

"Maybe Tora doesn't come here after all," said Zoe, stifling a yawn.

"We can't give up yet," said Ben. "Let's take turns sleeping. I'll take first watch."

"Thanks, but I'll never be able to sleep out here," protested Zoe, leaning against a tree trunk.

CHAPTER 7

TORA

The next thing Zoe knew, she was being shaken awake.

"Shh," whispered Ben. "Something's happening."

All the animals were standing alert. There was a faint rustling from the path. *WOOSH!* A sleek, dark shape stepped into the clearing and strode across the opening. In an instant, all the other animals fled.

The tiger moved steadily along in the dark, head held high, its muscles rippling with every step.

The silky fur, with its distinctive narrow stripes, gleamed in the faint moonlight.

"It's Tora," whispered Ben.

"She's beautiful," Zoe said with a sigh.

Tora padded silently toward the water, the black tip of her long tail curling up behind her.

All of a sudden, she stopped and sniffed the air. With a low growl, she came straight for their hiding place.

They heard a sound like water spraying. Then a pungent smell filled the air. Ben felt a trickle of warm, stinky urine squirt over his arm through the bush. Tora was leaving her scent!

"Gross!" Ben said under his breath. But he knew he had to stay still.

At last, Tora finished her business. She moved back toward the water.

Zoe chuckled. "At least we know the scent dispersers in our BUGs work!" whispered Zoe. "She didn't even know we were here."

"Wish it worked both ways," Ben whispered back, sniffing his arm. "This stinks!"

They peered through the leaves at Tora, who was now farther down the bank. She plunged into the water and swam, head high above the water. Then she got out, shook herself off, and began drinking deeply at the edge of the water.

"I bet she'll go hunting next," said Ben. "She'll have to take food back to her cubs."

"Then if we follow her, she should lead us to her den!" said Zoe. "Then we'll know where to go to check on the cubs."

Ben picked up his BUG. "I'll dart her."

He targeted Tora and fired at her left haunch. *PFFT!* The tiger's skin rippled. She flicked her tail as if she was swatting a fly.

Immediately, a satellite map of Silent
Water popped up on the BUG's screen. An
orange light flashed, showing the exact
position of the tiger.

Zoe parted the leaves again. "There's
something moving by Tora's legs, but it's
too blurry to make anything out," she said.
She carefully adjusted her zoom lens until
she could see clearly. Two little cubs were
playing at Tora's feet, padding each other
and rolling together at the edge of the water.

Ben gulped. "It looks like Uncle Stephen got his dates wrong," he said. "Those are Tora's cubs, and they're older than we thought. They're already out of the den!"

"Then they're in terrible danger," said Zoe. "And it's up to us to save them."

"Check where the poacher is," whispered Ben urgently.

Zoe checked the green light. "He hasn't moved from the village," she said. "We still have to tell Erika right away."

Zoe pressed the key on her BUG that would call Erika's phone. However, it just beeped quietly. "No signal here!" Zoe said. She groaned in frustration.

"The terrain here must be cutting off the signal," said Ben, keeping his voice down. "We need to get higher up to make a call."

"Well, I'm not climbing trees in the middle of the night!" argued Zoe.

"Don't worry," hissed Ben. "We'll just go to higher ground."

"Okay," Zoe agreed. "But Tora will hear us if we leave now. We'll just have to wait until she leaves."

"Lucky for you," teased Ben. "You can do some fluffy-wuffy little baby-cub watching. Meanwhile, I'm going to get some sleep." Ben laid down on the ground and propped his arm under his head.

Zoe eagerly focused her goggles on the cubs. "They're sooo cute!" she cooed softly. "Look at them wrestling with each other! And listen to them mew! I could just hug them all day long."

Ben sighed. He wouldn't get any sleep with Zoe making a fuss over the babies. Together, the twins watched Tora nudge her cubs toward the water. The baby tigers slurped water everywhere as they drank. Tora seemed to be keeping guard.

Tora held her head high and gave off soft, deep growls.

"She's a good mom," said Zoe. "She'll guard those babies with her life."

"Shh," warned Ben. "She's on the move."

Tora was padding silently toward the trail — and toward Ben and Zoe! They held their breath, hoping the scent dispersers in their BUGs were still working.

Zoe felt a mixture of thrill and terror as the beautiful tiger stalked along, her cubs padding softly at her heels.

They looked like they were trying to be as regal as their mother, but the cubs couldn't resist sniffing the ground or wrestling with each other as they went. Zoe gave a happy sigh as she watched.

Soon, they had disappeared. "Let's go," said Ben, stretching his stiff legs. "There's no time to lose."

"I'll find out exactly where the nearest high ground is," Zoe said. She checked her screen. "There it is. Cochoa Hill."

It was a long walk through the dark forest to Cochoa Hill. By the time they started the long trek up the steep slope, the first glimmers of sun were beginning to filter through the trees.

"I hope we get a signal up there," panted Zoe, pushing through the huge flowers and green undergrowth.

"The sooner WILD can contact the sanctuary, the better," Zoe said.

Finally, they reached the top of the hill. Ben wiped the sweat off his forehead and sipped the last of his water.

"Got a signal!" yelled Zoe, sending a flock of bright yellow birds screeching into the air.

She paused. "Nope, now it's gone again," Zoe said. "And we've run out of hill to climb."

Ben grunted. "Looks like I'm gonna be doing some tree climbing," he said grimly. Ben looped the strap of his BUG round his wrist and began to shimmy up the nearest tree. He used the dangling creeper vines to pull himself up, ignoring the ants that were running all over his arms.

"Be careful," warned Zoe. "I don't want you falling on top of me."

Ben smiled. As he climbed, the forest grew darker and huge drops of water began to splatter down through the trees. Soon, every other jungle sound was blocked out by the beat of the water on the canopy above. Ben could feel the tree swaying under his weight as he gripped it with one hand.

With the other hand, he fumbled with his BUG, trying to use it. Rainwater was streaming down the trunk, making it hard to hold on. *Hope this thing's waterproof,* he thought as he struggled with the slippery buttons.

At last, Ben accessed the communicator. He tapped the key to call Erika and held the BUG to his ear. It rang and rang.

Ben pressed 1 to get through to WILD headquarters instead. "Hello?" he shouted as he heard a faint voice. The signal seemed to be coming and going. "Uncle Stephen?" No answer. Still holding the device to his ear, Ben tried to scramble higher up, pushing on the spindly branches with his feet.

"Tora's cubs are out of the den," he shouted. "And the poachers are in the village — at least we think so."

"Can you contact the sanctuary for us?" Ben shouted. "Are you there, WILD HQ?!"

"Hello, Ben!" He could barely hear his uncle's cheerful voice. "Bad signal. Say again?"

Ben heaved himself up as high as he could. "We need Sanctuary to come now!" he said. "The cubs are —"

CRACK! The branch under his foot snapped. Ben plummeted downward.

He grabbed wildly at the trunk as he flew past. Wet twigs slapped his face and he felt the skin being scraped from his palms.

Ben couldn't grab anything. Just when he thought he was doomed, the BUG strap around his wrist got caught on a branch. He jerked to a disorienting halt.

He found himself swinging twenty feet above the ground, dazed but unhurt. His arm felt as if it was going to be pulled out of its socket, but at least he'd stopped falling.

The BUG suddenly vibrated. "Ben?" It was Uncle Stephen's voice. "Are you there? How's it going?"

Typical, thought Ben. *I'm hanging from a tree in a tropical rainstorm and now I get perfect reception!*

"Urgent message!" he shouted up to the BUG. "Tora's cubs are out of the den."

"Already?!" he heard Uncle Stephen exclaim. "Tell me all about them. Do they have —" The BUG chirped, then went silent.

Ben managed to haul himself up onto the branch. He unhooked the BUG and climbed down the tree.

Zoe was hiding underneath one of the tree's huge leaves.

"Are you okay?" Zoe yelled over the sound of the pounding rain.

"I slipped a little," Ben said. He grinned, showing her his palms.

Zoe grimaced. "Nasty," she said. "Did you speak to Uncle Stephen?"

"For a second," Ben said. "I just hope he got my message."

Zoe swung her backpack off her shoulder and found the medical kit. She splashed distilled water on his grazes and began to cover them with bandages.

"Better get back to the village," said Ben. "I think we should make sure that — ow!"

Zoe nodded. "Yes, yes — make sure the poachers aren't on the tiger's trail yet," she said with a smile. "Just hold still, you big baby."

CHAPTER 8

CATUR

It was late morning by the time Ben and Zoe reached the village. It had stopped raining, and everything was steaming in the sun.

"At least the rain washed the tiger pee off," joked Zoe. "You were really starting to smell."

"Very funny," Ben said. "Can we get something to eat now? If anyone hears my stomach rumbling, they'll think the tiger has already arrived in town."

"After we've checked on the poachers," Zoe said. She tapped some keys on her BUG. A green light flashed. "That Wicaksono guy is still at home. Maybe we can get close enough to hear him talk."

They snuck toward his house. There was no sign of anyone outside, but there was a row of men's shoes by the door. They could hear a voice coming from inside.

"Deal again, I'm feeling lucky," one said. "Get your money ready."

"Sounds like they're playing cards," said Zoe.

"That's risky," said Ben. "The TV show I saw earlier said that gambling is forbidden in Sumatra."

A woman walked briskly toward the house.

Zoe and Ben quickly ducked down and pretended to be playing games on their BUGs. The woman didn't seem to see them. She marched straight up the steps.

"Sapto!" she called out in an angry voice. "I know you're in there!" She thumped on the wooden door. "I'm staying here until you come out."

There was a shuffling from inside. The woman knocked on the door again. At last it opened. Wicaksono stood in the doorway. "Ah, hello, Ratu," he said. "Your husband isn't here. I haven't seen him today —"

The woman pushed past him. "Out of my way!" she growled, entering the house.

Ben and Zoe could hear yelling and things being knocked over. Then the woman reappeared, dragging a man along by his ear.

"Some husband you are!" she yelled. She pulled him down the steps. "You promised to stop gambling. You lied to me!"

"I'm sorry, Ratu, my love," the man whimpered. "I was just about to win! I had the best cards ever. I would have bought you a brand new — ow!"

Two other men came to the door of the hut. They pulled on their shoes and scurried away shyly.

Ben looked at Zoe. "Those guys aren't deadly poachers!" he said. "They were just a couple of guys playing a secret gambling game. 'Making a killing' just meant winning at cards."

Zoe sighed. "We're back to square one," she said. "What do we do now?"

"Angkasa knew about the poachers," Ben replied. "Maybe we can ask her a few more questions without scaring her off."

They walked through the village, but there was no sign of Angkasa's fruit stall today.

"What have you done to yourself?" said a voice. They spun around to see Catur.

He came out of his shop and took Ben's palms in his hands, looking concerned.

"I . . . slipped and fell," said Ben, only half lying.

"I can sell you something to make it heal," Catur said. He gestured toward his shop. "Come inside."

Ben and Zoe followed him in. Beads and brooches and carved wooden animals were displayed on a long table next to a row of bottles of richly colored powders and pills.

There were some rings displayed on the back wall beside a curtained door. Zoe went over to have a look. She knew Grandma would like them.

Catur picked up a small pot of bright red ointment. "This is a salve made from the lipstick tree. It helps to keep wounds clean."

Catur opened the lid and let Ben sniff at it.

As Zoe examined the rings she had a sudden idea. Catur might know something about the man that Angkasa had mentioned. But how could she bring up the subject of poaching without explaining why they wanted to know?

"This ointment is very good," Catur was saying. "But if you are willing to pay a bit more, I have something . . . special . . . in my storeroom." He gestured toward the curtain. "Guaranteed to heal those wounds quickly. I usually don't tell tourists about it, but I like you two."

Alarm bells started ringing in Zoe's head. What did Catur mean by "special"? She exchanged a quick glance with Ben.

She could see Ben had the same suspicion as she did. Was Catur the "bad man" Angkasa had told them about? Was he dealing in animal parts and making ointments out of tiger bones?

"We don't have much money on us at the moment," Zoe said. "So we'll go with the salve."

"Of course," said Catur smoothly. "But do come back if you need something . . . stronger."

* * *

As soon as they'd left the shop, Ben pulled Zoe into the gap between two of the wooden houses. "He's up to no good," Ben muttered. "I can feel it."

"You've got that smile on your face again," said Zoe. "What are you planning?"

"It sounds like Catur could be linked to the poachers," Ben told her. "But we have to make sure we've got the right man this time."

"And how do you plan to do that?" demanded Zoe. "We can't just ask him."

"I'm going to get a look inside that storeroom," said Ben. "Let's see if there's another way inside."

They crept through compost piles and chicken droppings until they came to the back of Catur's shop. "There's a door," said Ben. "Now here's your part in the plan. Go in the front and keep him busy while I search his storeroom," Ben said.

"Okay," said Zoe. "But remember what Uncle Stephen said — the poachers are dangerous."

Ben nodded.

"See you in a minute," Zoe said, darting off.

Ben waited until he heard Zoe's voice from inside the store. "I can't decide," she was saying loudly. "Could you take them out here so I can get a better look in the light?"

Smart girl, Ben thought. *Now that Catur's distracted . . .*

Ben carefully opened the back door of the shop and crept inside. The storeroom was hot and gloomy, lit only by a small, dirty window.

There were shelves piled high with containers and packets. Ben inspected them all. It was just the ordinary stock for the shop. He pulled out some cans of baked beans to see if there was anything hidden there, but he found only a few dead flies.

Ben could hear Zoe chattering on. "The green one is nice," she said.

Ben noticed a shabby chest of drawers in the corner. He pulled open the top drawer, wincing as it squeaked. It was full of jars and boxes. Ben picked up a small glass bottle, containing what looked like strands of wire. Then he opened a box and nearly dropped it in shock. It was full of dried eyeballs!

Gross! he thought. He put the box back in the drawer and noticed something. *Those aren't wires,* he thought. *They're whiskers!*

Farther back in the drawer, he saw something rolled up in brown paper. He uncurled an edge and found himself staring at a beautiful orange and black striped pelt.

Then he heard a muffled voice from the shop. "I want to talk to you, Catur!" the voice said. "Come with me."

The translated words rang in Ben's ear. That wasn't Zoe speaking, it was a man. And his footsteps were heading across the wooden floor of the shop, straight toward the storeroom!

There was no time to get out. Ben had to hide. He squeezed into the tiny gap between the chest of drawers and the wall just as the curtain was flung aside. He realized he'd left the drawer open, but it was too late to close it.

"You shouldn't be seen with me," he heard Catur snap.

"I wouldn't be here if you'd told me what is happening," the other man said.

"When we didn't hear from you," the voice said, "I started to worry that you were planning to do the job alone and take all the money for yourself."

Catur didn't respond. The man raised his voice and let out a cold laugh. "If so," he growled, "then we'd have had to take care of you as well as the tiger."

Ben listened carefully.

"You're crazy," Catur said, laughing. "How could I cheat you, my friend? We're all in this together. We're like brothers! Meet me at the usual place at nightfall and I'll tell you the plan. Now go."

And we're going to be there to hear it, too, thought Ben. He heard the stranger barge his way out of the back door. *But Catur is coming this way!*

Ben tried to edge farther back, but there was nowhere to go. He was going to be caught.

THUMP! Catur slammed the drawer shut and stomped back into his shop. Ben sagged with relief. He eased himself out of his hiding place, peered around the door to make sure the coast was clear, and slipped back outside.

He zipped around to the front of the shop. "Hurry up, Zoe," he said, pretending to be annoyed at his sister's shopping.

"I'll be back later," Zoe told Catur. Moments later, she bounded out to join Ben. "Is he a poacher?" she whispered once they were outside.

Ben nodded. "And we're going to follow him tonight and find out his plans."

Zoe grinned. "Stakeout time!"

CHAPTER 9

STAKEOUT!

The sun was low over the trees when Catur locked up his shop. He hurried along a path toward the forest. Zoe quickly aimed the tracker, but Ben put his hand on her arm. "Too risky," he said. "We can't do anything that might alert him. He's smart, this one."

Keeping to the shadows, they followed the poacher's bobbing flashlight. It was dark by the time Catur came to a rough hut, half covered in vines.

Ben and Zoe crouched down behind a pitcher plant, its large, cup-like leaves heavy with water. They slipped on their night goggles and put in their earphones so that they could hear the translated conversation. Two men were waiting for Catur on the porch.

"That tall, mean-looking one with the big nose was the man in the shop," whispered Zoe.

"The short one doesn't look any nicer," Ben replied. "We have to be extra careful."

As soon as the men went inside the hut, Ben and Zoe crept up and hid underneath a window.

"I've been to the den," came Catur's voice. "It was empty. So the cubs are out. This is the moment we've been waiting for."

"We must act quickly before the Sanctuary gets wind of it and whisks them away to safety," Catur added.

"Then we'll do it tonight," said the man from the shop. "Our client won't pay us if we fail."

"We won't fail," Catur said, sounding confident. "I've already dug a hole for the trap at Silent Water where the tiger always drinks. We'll set the trap and bait it with the goat we bought. I smeared the goat in tiger dung, so that will scare off any other animals. After the trap is set, we'll return here and wait. The moment the trap is sprung, an alarm will sound on my remote, and we'll go grab the tigers."

"Why don't we wait there for her?" the third man asked. "We don't want to miss our chance."

"Don't be stupid," said Catur. "She'd smell us before we even knew she was there. No, my friends, my way is the best way. We trap them, then shoot them. A tiger in a cage is an easy target. But be careful where you aim. We don't want to damage their skins!"

Zoe stared at Ben in horror. "They're killing the tigers tonight," she whispered.

"The sanctuary won't get here in time to save them!" Ben added.

"That was a smart idea you had, Catur, putting out scary stories about Silent Water," the first man said. "How did you dream that up?"

"I didn't have to," Catur answered. "There have always been legends about the danger of Silent Water. I just repeated the stories so the villagers would keep clear of the area."

"You've never seen anything there, have you?" the third man asked. His voice sounded shaky.

"Never!" scoffed Catur. "Are you chickening out on us?"

"Of course not!" the man said.

Just then, Ben's stomach gurgled loudly. "Be quiet!" hissed Zoe.

"I can't help it," Ben whispered. "We've missed a few meals today and I'm hungry." He began to dig through his pockets.

"What are you doing now?" Zoe asked.

"I have an apple in here somewhere," Ben said. "There it is — oops!"

The apple tumbled out and bounced loudly on the wooden porch, and then rolled into the long grass.

Ben and Zoe froze.

"What was that?" came a gruff voice from inside the hut. "Is there someone outside?"

Chairs were scraped back and heavy footsteps made for the door.

"Hide!" whispered Zoe.

They jumped off the porch and into the bushes. The three men were out of the hut now, shining flashlights around. Ben and Zoe tried to go deeper among the trees, but it was impossible to move without making a noise.

"There — can you hear it?" Catur called out. He moved his light over the grass. The beam swept just above Ben and Zoe's heads. Ben felt something on his boot. He looked down and stifled a gasp.

A coral snake was slithering silently over the laces! He closed his eyes and held his breath. *Think of something else,* he thought, sweating. *Just stay still.* But all he could think about was that the venom of the coral snake was deadly. He had to look.

He opened his eyes to see the venomous snake's tail disappear into the undergrowth.

Ben let out a relieved sigh.

"Over there!" shouted Catur. "I heard something." Catur fixed his flashlight firmly on the bushes in front of them.

"I've got an idea," Zoe whispered urgently. "Bring up the sound file of the tarsier monkey's call on your BUG."

Ben clicked his BUG's keys, turning the volume to FULL. Then, he clicked PLAY. A shrill cry filled the air. At the same time, Zoe flicked a switch on her BUG, creating a hologram of two tarsier monkeys.

"What was that?" Big Nose said, glancing about.

"Tarsiers," said Catur, swinging his flashlight upward. "Look up in the trees."

The first man swung his weapon around and aimed it at the monkeys hanging in the trees.

"Don't waste your ammo," said Catur. "Save it for the tigers."

Zoe grabbed Ben's hand. "These poachers are evil," she whispered.

"Come on," Catur said. "Let's go put the trap in place."

The poachers trudged away to their shack. They reappeared carrying a large metal cage between them and set off. Soon the forest went back to its usual drone of insects and distant animal cries.

"Nice decoy, Zoe," said Ben. "Let's follow them. We've got to spring the trap before Tora gets there with her cubs."

"That won't work," said Zoe.

"It'll set off the poachers' alarm and bring them running to reset it," Zoe said. She checked the tiger's whereabouts on her BUG. "Tora's pretty far away right now, south of Silent Water, and not moving. We're to the west."

Ben nodded, anticipating his sister's plan. "Then we'll cross her path and scare her off before she gets anywhere near the trap," he said.

"Exactly!" Zoe said. "Let's go!"

CHAPTER 10

TRAPPED!

They hadn't gone far when Zoe noticed that the blip on her BUG screen had started to blink. "Tora's on the move!" she said. "She's going to get to the trap before we can head her off."

"Then we don't have a choice," said Ben, stopping in his tracks. "We have to get to the trap and block it before the poachers get to it."

"Great idea!" said Zoe.

Ben grinned. "I know," he said.

They dashed through the forest toward the watering hole, twigs cracking loudly underfoot. "Hope the poachers don't hear us coming," Zoe panted as they ran.

"We'll just have to take that chance," said Ben. "Look! We're here now, and it looks like the poachers are gone."

They came to a criss-cross pattern of large and small pawprints in the soft dirt. "They had to have put the trap near these tiger tracks," Ben said.

They pushed aside bushes and ferns, desperately searching for the trap. Ben came to a mass of creeper vines. As he pulled at them, his foot clanged against something hard and metallic.

"Found it," Ben called. He kneeled and carefully removed some of the leaves.

A cage made of shiny sheet metal was set in the ground. The barred door was raised, ready to drop. He could hear the sad bleat of the live goat inside.

Zoe joined him. Then something caught her eye. "Look, Ben!" Zoe said. She pointed toward a huge tiger skin that had been draped over a nearby branch. "That's what Catur meant about keeping other animals away. They'll all steer clear of that, especially now that it has Tora's scent all over it."

She checked the orange light on her BUG. "Oh, no," she said urgently. "She's almost here. We've got to block the trap!" Zoe glanced around desperately. "There must be some fallen branches we can lay across the opening or something," she said.

"There's no time!" Ben cried.

"Then we have to spring the trap and chase Tora away," said Zoe.

But then the twins noticed a slight movement. They both spun around. Tora was standing on the opposite bank, her cubs near her feet.

"Tora's here!" Zoe whispered, pushing Ben down into the undergrowth beside the cage. "I don't think she's seen us yet."

The tiger raised her head and sniffed the air. Her tail swished back and forth.

"She can smell the goat," whispered Ben.

"But not us!" Zoe pulled out her BUG. "Luckily, our scent dispersers are still active."

The cubs suddenly bounded around the bank. With a low growl, Tora splashed through the water and blocked them.

"The tigers are heading for the trap," Zoe whispered, almost in tears. "We've got to do something!"

"There's only one thing we can do!" cried Ben. Zoe could see Ben had that wild look in his eyes. Before Zoe could stop him, he jumped into the metal cage!

CLANG! The trap slammed shut over his head. At the harsh metallic sound, Tora reared up with a frightened snarl, and the cubs leaped away in terror. In an instant, they all disappeared into the shadows.

"It worked!" cried Zoe in relief. "Nice moves, Ben."

"Now get me out," called Ben as the goat nuzzled his ear. "The poachers will be here any minute."

Zoe pulled on the trap door. "I can't open it!" she said in alarm. "Try from the inside."

Ben pushed on the door. Nothing happened.

Zoe picked up a fallen branch and tried to pry it open, but the branch snapped in half. She ran around the edge of the waterhole and found a sharp rock.

"Cover your face," she warned.

Zoe brought the rock down with all her strength. It shattered into fragments, leaving the locking mechanism barely scratched.

"I can't break it," said Zoe in despair. "There must be something else I can do . . ."

But it was too late. The sound of voices came through the trees. The poachers were on their way.

"Run, Zoe!" Ben yelled.

"I'm not leaving you!" his sister said.

"But you'll get caught too!" Ben said. "Run!"

"Shut up a minute," Zoe said. "I'm thinking."

"There's no time to think!" Ben said frantically. "Go!"

Zoe's eyes burst open. "I've got it!" she said. Just as the poachers reached the clearing, she slipped out of sight.

"Check the area," ordered Catur. "They might not all be caught in the trap."

"It's clear," another man said. "We've got the little beauties."

There was the click of a gun being cocked. "Time to get rid of them," Catur said.

"Good thing they're quiet," the third man said nastily. "Easier to kill that way."

Zoe pressed a button on her BUG. An unearthly wailing sound echoed through the clearing. Through a tiny gap in the creeper vines she could see the men freeze at the sound.

"What's that?" one of the men squeaked. He looked fidgety and nervous.

His gun was shaking as he tried to keep it steady. "Is it . . . is it —" the man started.

"Come on," interrupted Catur. "It's just some harmless animal. You're wasting time."

The men approached the trap with nervous steps. So Zoe set the BUG's volume even louder. But it was no use. The men were crouching down, their guns held against their shoulders. Zoe knew that any second they would see Ben.

Suddenly, a deep rhythmic knocking sound came from the trap. The men stumbled back. One man dropped his gun. "That's no tiger!" he gasped. "The locals are right — this place is haunted!"

"Don't be stupid," said Catur. "You're just getting spooked by the animal cries."

A horrible groaning sound echoed inside the metal trap. Big Nose shined his flashlight down into it with a quivering hand. "Look at those huge shining eyes!" he whispered. Then the words *orang pendek, orang pendek* rose in a ghostly howl.

"I can't stay here!" yelled one of the men. He turned to run.

"Me, either!" wailed another. He dashed into the forest.

And just like that, Catur was all alone. "Is this some kind of trick?" he muttered through gritted teeth, stalking toward the cage. "There's no such thing as an orang pendek."

Zoe held her breath as he shined his flashlight through the cage. "What the —?" Catur yelled. He sprang back in surprise. Then he laughed grimly.

"Huge shining eyes?" he said. "It's just a kid in goggles! Wait a minute . . . I know you!"

Catur's voice had a violent edge to it. "You're in big trouble, little boy," he said. Then he released the trap mechanism and the door sprang open.

Zoe felt around until her hands closed on a heavy stick. As she tensed her muscles to attack, a loud roar froze her to the spot. She watched as Catur swung around to confront Tora! The tiger stood on the bank, her shoulders raised and her teeth bared.

Catur whimpered. Tora crouched, ready to spring, as Catur aimed his gun.

"NO!" shrieked Zoe.

The sound of a bullet firing rang out.

Tora slumped to the ground. She tried to raise herself up, but she fell heavily onto her side. Her tail swished weakly and her head sank slowly onto the muddy ground. A moment later, she was completely still.

The clearing was suddenly full of shouts and circling lights. The next moment, Catur vanished into the forest. Zoe reached a hand out to Ben, tears streaming down her face.

"What's going on?" Ben gasped. He quickly climbed out of the trap.

Zoe flung her arms around her brother. "I'm so glad you're okay!" she sobbed. Then she pointed at Tora's lifeless body down along the bank. "But we couldn't save her."

Just then, a woman ran up to them.

She was wearing a green uniform with an elephant logo on it. "What are you kids doing here?" she asked in an Australian accent.

"We met a shopkeeper in Aman Tempat who had some illegally poached stuff," Ben explained. "He said his name was Catur. We overheard him talking about killing a tiger, so we followed him. We would've told our aunt who's staying with us, but there was no time and we didn't know who else to trust. We managed to keep the tiger away from his trap, but . . ."

Zoe raised her tear-filled eyes and finished her brother's sentence. "But we were too late to save her," she said.

"Too late?" said the woman. "What are you talking about? Pat yourselves on the back, because you just saved this tiger's life!"

Zoe's jaw dropped. "But the man shot her!" she cried. "She's dead."

"Tora's not dead, silly," the woman said, smiling. "That fool of a poacher never even fired his gun. Go feel her chest. She's still breathing."

Zoe dashed over to the fallen tiger. She pressed her hand gently against the beast's chest. "She's right!" Zoe cried with glee.

"But how?" Ben asked. "We heard a gunshot, and then Tora fell to the ground."

"That was me," said the woman. "I fired a tranquilizer dart at her."

"Who are you?" Ben asked.

The woman held out her hand. "My name's Barbara," she said. "I'm with the Kinaree Sanctuary. We got an anonymous message saying there was a mother tiger and cubs in danger. But I didn't expect to find a couple of kids under fire as well!"

Zoe stroked Tora's magnificent fur. "Look at her noble face," said Zoe, smiling. "Her markings are so beautiful, the white around her muzzle and over her eyes."

"I don't get it," said Barbara, shaking her head. "We had no idea about this tiger and her cubs until we got the phone call."

Ben's eyes widened with concern. "Wait, where are the cubs?" he asked.

"Barbara!" someone called out.

Ben and Zoe looked over to see Wicaksono, the gambler from the village, carrying one of the cubs. Another man came behind with the second cub, and a third led the goat along by a length of rope.

"We're lucky to have Wicaksono here," Barbara said. "He's the best animal trapper I know."

Ben and Zoe looked at each other. "You come see," Wicaksono said, beckoning them closer.

A few feet away, the cubs mewed as Wicaksono handed one of them to Zoe. It licked her hand and nuzzled her fingers with its head.

Zoe wiped her eyes on her sleeves. She gave the tiger a gentle hug.

"You're going to be all right," she whispered. Its big round eyes gazed up.

Four men came forward with a wooden cage pulled on a cart. The sleeping Tora was lifted very carefully and placed inside.

"Back to the village," said Barbara. "We'll come back for that horrible metal contraption later."

"What about this?" called a man, holding up the tiger skin in disgust.

"Bring that with us," Barbara said. "We'll need it for evidence."

The morning light trickled through the trees as the group followed the cart out of the forest. Wicaksono walked with Barbara and asked questions about Tora's health.

"How could we have thought he was a poacher?" Zoe whispered to Ben as the little cub nuzzled her chin. "He obviously loves animals."

"We shouldn't have jumped to conclusions so quickly," Ben agreed.

"Catur seemed so nice when we first met him," Zoe said, "and we were wrong about him, too."

"Should we let Wicaksono know that we tagged him?" Ben asked.

"We can't," said Zoe. "Then we'd have to tell him about WILD. They seem to believe we're just tourists who stumbled across this horrible plot. It won't hurt him."

Back at the village, the wooden cage was winched on to the back of the sanctuary's truck. The cubs were put into a smaller box.

Zoe and Ben stroked Tora's fur through the bars as she slept. "Goodbye," said Zoe. "You're going to a lovely new home where you and your children can be safe."

Barbara came over to join them. "Tora's cubs will need names," she said. "Do either of you have any suggestions? They're a boy and girl."

Zoe opened her mouth, but Ben spoke up before she could. "Don't you dare suggest Fluffy and Wuffy!" Ben joked, grinning.

Zoe punched her brother in the arm. "Very funny," she said.

Barbara laughed. "What are your names?" she asked. "I think we'll name them after you, since you seem to fight with your sibling like the cubs do."

"Ben and Zoe," they said together.

Barbara smiled. "Perfect!" she said.

"So what happens next?" asked Ben.

"Our vet will do an examination and
tag them, like you do dogs and cats,"
said Barbara. "Then they'll be set free in
the reserve. Hopefully the mother will
re-establish her territory and live a long and
happy life. There's a male there already, so
she may have more cubs in the future —
which is what we need if we're going to save
the Sumatran tigers from extinction."

She paid the villagers for their help, and
climbed into the cab of the truck. Then she
leaned out of the window, waving a notepad
at Ben and Zoe.

"Write your email addresses on here,"
Barbara said. "I'll send you an update."

"And what about the poachers?" asked Zoe as she wrote. "There was Catur and two others, and they're still free."

"That shop over there is where Catur's selling animal parts," added Ben, pointing.

Barbara smiled. "I'll tell the police," she said. "Those villains will soon know what it's like to be hunted!"

With that, the truck drove off. Ben and Zoe watched until it bumped out of sight in the early morning sunshine. Tora and her cubs were on their way to a safe new home.

"Things turned out pretty good today," Ben said as they walked through the market.

Zoe grinned. "You know what's really good about today?" she asked.

"We can get some food now?" guessed Ben.

"No," said Zoe, giving him a friendly shove. "That collector will have to do without her family of stuffed tigers!"

Ben laughed. "I hope Erika's found some info on her," he said.

Zoe nodded. "That would be perfect," she said. She thought for a moment, and added, "Of course, we won't be able to put any of this on our website."

"It would make a great blog post," agreed Ben. "Too bad we have to keep it all secret."

Zoe's stomach grumbled. "I'm starving."

"For once we're in agreement!" Ben said. "I wasn't joking about finding some food."

Zoe laughed. Ben pulled out his BUG. "But first things first, we should let Uncle Stephen know about Tora." He pressed the key for WILD HQ.

"Look at you, being responsible for once," Zoe joked. "And *before* you've eaten!"

Just then, a voice rang out through Ben's BUG. "Hello, Ben," Uncle Stephen said. "Is everything all right? Has our friend been moved safely to her new home?"

"Yes," answered Ben simply. He was dying to tell his uncle every detail of the adventure, but he knew it had to wait. He couldn't risk being overheard. "Can't talk now."

"I understand," Uncle Stephen said happily. "I knew I could count on you!"

Zoe and Ben exchanged proud glances as Stephen went on. "And Erika's had a successful mission, too!" he said. "I'm sure she'll tell you all about it when she picks you up tomorrow."

"That's great news!" Zoe said.

"Indeed," said their uncle. "I'll see you back at HQ for a debriefing." Then the connection was cut.

"Uncle Stephen will probably give us a new mission when we see him," said Ben as they walked back to their hut. "I wonder what it'll be."

"I know one thing about it," said Zoe. "It's gonna be WILD!"

THE AUTHORS

Jan Burchett and **Sara Vogler** were already
friends when they discovered they both wanted
to write children's books, and that it was much
more fun to do it together. They have since written
over a hundred and thirty stories ranging from
educational books and stories for younger readers
to young adult fiction. They have written for series
such as Dinosaur Cove and Beast Quest, and they
are authors of the Gargoylz books.

THE ILLUSTRATOR

Diane Le Feyer discovered a passion for drawing
and animation at the age of five. In 2002, she
graduated with honors from the Ecole Emile Cohl
school of design. Diane worked as a character
designer, 3D modeler, and animator in the video
games industry before joining the Cartoon Saloon
animation studio, where she worked as a director,
animator, illustrator, and character designer. Diane
was also a part of the early design and development
of the movie *The Secret of Kells*.

GLOSSARY

composing (kuhm-POZE-ing)—if you are composing yourself, you are returning to a calm and normal state

critically (KRIT-uh-kuhl-ee)—extremely and dangerously

debrief (dee-BREEF)—a meeting in which a person gives information to their superiors after a mission is completed

endangered (en-DAYN-jurd)—at risk of going extinct

glimmers (GLIM-urz)—shines faintly

habitat (HAB-uh-tat)—the place and natural conditions in which a plant or animal lives

intel (IN-tel)—information

mission (MISH-uhn)—a special job or task

operative (OP-ur-uh-tiv)—a secret agent

sanctuary (SANGK-choo-er-ee)—a natural area where animals are protected from hunters

undergrowth (UHN-dur-grohth)—plants that grow beneath the tall, mature trees in a forest

villains (VIL-uhnz)—wicked or evil people

THE TIGER
STATUS: CRITICALLY ENDANGERED

Almost ninety-five percent of the world's population of tigers has been lost in the past 100 years! There are less than 4,000 tigers living in the wild today. Several threats have contributed to their dwindling numbers:

POACHING: Poachers kill animals and sell their body parts. Poaching of tigers is banned worldwide, but some poachers continue to kill and sell the various breeds of nearly extinct tigers.

DEFORESTATION: Some areas of rainforest are logged illegally in order to sell the wood and land. The land is also cleared by corporations looking to build oil palm plantations. The destruction of the rainforest means tigers have a harder time finding prey or food. With their habitat shrinking, tigers wander near villages, where they risk being shot.

HUNTING: Sadly, there are still humans who hunt and kill tigers for the pleasure or thrill of the kill.

BUT IT'S NOT ALL BAD NEWS FOR TIGERS! The Sumatran Tiger Trust is fighting for the future of the Sumatran tiger. Their tiger preservation team captures and re-releases tigers into safe areas. They also locate tigers and alert the Indonesian government so it can outlaw logging in areas where the tiger population is high.

DISCUSSION QUESTIONS

1. Ben and Zoe do their best to protect endangered animals. What kinds of things can you do to help animals and the environment? Talk about it.

2. Are Ben and Zoe heroes for helping animals in need? Why or why not?

3. There are many illustrations in this book. Which one is your favorite? Why?

WRITING PROMPTS

1. Imagine that you're a tiger. Write a short story about your life as a tiger. What do you do in the rainforest where you live? What do you eat? How do you survive? Write about being a tiger.

2. Various traps are used in this book. Design your own trap that is used to safely and painlessly capture a large animal. How does it work? What materials will you need to build it? Write about your trap, and then draw a picture of it.

3. What adventure do Zoe and Ben have next? Imagine your own Wild Rescue story and write a chapter about their next mission.

J

Burchett, Jan.

Poacher panic.